Stir my Heart... Still my Soul

"At times may be it isn't about 'we', But it is about 'thee.'"

PARVESH CHANDEL

FROG BOOKS

First published in India 2014 by Frog Books
An imprint of Leadstart Publishing Pvt Ltd
1 Level, Trade Centre
Bandra Kurla Complex
Bandra (East) Mumbai 400 051 India
Telephone: +91-22-40700804
Fax: +91-22-40700800
Email: info@leadstartcorp.com
www.leadstartcorp.com / www.frogbooks.net

Sales Office:
Unit No.25/26, Building No.A/1,
Near Wadala RTO,
Wadala (East), Mumbai - 400037 India
Phone: +91 22 24046887

US Office:
Axis Corp, 7845 E Oakbrook Circle
Madison, WI 53717 USA

ISBN 978-93-84226-90-9

Book Editor: Cora Bhatia
Design Editor: Mishta Roy
Layout: Chandravadan R. Shiroorkar

Typeset in Book Antiqua
Printed at Dhote Offset Technokrafts Pvt. Ltd., Mumbai

Price – India: Rs 100; Elsewhere: US $4

About the Author

Hailed from the hills and spent his entire life in Chandigarh, Parvesh Chandel is an author. With his unveiling novel, 'Stir My Heart, Still My Soul', he took his first stride into the world of the narrative. Parvesh Chandel graduated from Goswami Ganesh Dutta Sanatan Dharam College, Chandigarh. He holds Masters in Mass Communication and Journalism from Panjab University, Chandigarh and he was ardently active in politics all through his University days. He was designated as the President of Akhil Bhartiya Vidyarathi Parishad. Being a writer was his dream. He did what he believed, excelled or not, a veiled hidden story about to be unveiled. Thinking beyond a particular genre, he penned down about something or anything, which evokes him less as an individual and more as a human. He started his career in advertising and then left it to pursue his passion for writing. A self- proclaimed eccentric, he loves to play cricket. He is voracious, witty and loves life.

He can be reached at parveshchandel@yahoo.com

Dedication

To the people who created me and to the feeling that would not have induced me, had the book not been there in your hands

Acknowledgements

A book may be written by a sole being, but a book is a creation of many people unswervingly or unreliably. And if I move further without paying gratitude to them, this would be an injustice to the labour and skills of many, whose names are not acknowledged, would portray me as a self-centred human, which I doubt I am. So dear readers, here are the people who made this novel a reality. Devoid of these people, I would have not been able to write my novel.

- Above all I would thank, but will fail to pay back the love, support of my parents and alma mater, who bestowed their blessings, as we all know:

गुरुर्ब्रह्मा गुरुर्विष्णुः गुरुर्देवो महेश्वरः ।

गूरुरेव परंब्रह्म तस्मै श्रीगूरवे नमः ॥

- Gurpreet and Serena, rollin' rats, who supported and encouraged me, in spite of all the time they had to invest in me. It was their constant interference that helped me make it what this novel is today. It is an effort which has come true ☺

- Heartily thanks to Rashim Chandel for suggesting and persisting with Leadstart.

- Time is a greatest gift anybody can give you; again I thank Ruchi from the bottom of my heart for investing her time and to ensure these become success moments.

- My editor, the designing team and Leadstart Publications Pvt. Ltd. to lend me a hand sharing my inner thoughts with the rest of the world.

- My readers, who gave me truly such an honour by picking my book and adding it to their shelves. I assure you many more opportunities to put forth my credentials as an author.

- Last and not the least, Shaurya, my nephew, for allowing me the name as a protagonist and I beg forgiveness of all those who have been with me over the course of the years and whose names I have failed to mention.

Contents

इश्क़ -ए-अफ़साना, ईमान-ए –इश्क़

"Love is supreme. Ergo, neither love nor we can fail in love, but what and where we fail is in, expressing the idea of love."

Chapter 1

How I met her…

Astute; student political leader…

Perplexed; every time looking at nature's beauty (women)…

Hay wire; in the belief of love…

Undoubtedly, a fervent admirer of lovely women…

Surprisingly politically incorrect politician…

But, nonetheless as we say, change is inevitable. And history has been great evidence that time will change.

Time might get bad to worse, or maybe, from worse to best but, it will.

Similarly, nothing usual it was, change that was to come, was with a different start, for me in a very unique way, to change not only my personality but even the belief.

I realized characteristics, nature, thoughts, everything can change. And, so, it happened.

It wasn't a feast of eyes but a melody of ears, which was a decisive factor for a change that was coming my way.

However, as I was involved in serious student politics for more than five years now, and this year (i.e.2012), being presidential candidate for my party, my phone ringing sixty times in one hour was no surprise and no different, but the day I still remember 12th June, became unexpectedly to be a very special day.

I had to get my party's president (i.e. me) posters printed. And so for the same reason was to talk over phone with the girl, who I had, no idea would be the love of my life.

And the girl was from the Law Department, who was nominated as the Vice-President by the party senior members.

So, I was asked to get her posters as well. As, her photograph was also required for the posters. I was supposed to call her. So, here comes a sudden cyclone, which I never knew would change me as a package.

Though, I was the presidential candidate of my party but I have always been scared and hence, an introvert as far as 'initiating' talks with girls was concerned. Although, I always had a huge group of around sixteen close friends, out of them fifteen were female friends and an only male friend. Shockingly or surprisingly, out of those fifteen, unpredictably thirteen love me and so that was the reason I believed love in market is easy to buy. I have until this point never loved anybody and had never even ever initiated any kind of talks with girls, neither in School nor in College and surely not in University. But then, here I had no choice, but to call her.

I called her.

Her phone rang. (*tring tring…*)

Unfortunately, fortunately, the moment she lifted and started speaking, her tone proved me she is a law student and she is not at all sorry for being so curt.

I said, "Hey, hi, this is Shaurya," and further requested, "Please give me your photograph as it is required for the posters."

"I am in the bus right now. I am travelling and would be in the bus for next four more hours. And moreover, I need to get it clicked. Wait for another four hours or rather go ahead without mine. Text me your e-mail id and make sure don't call again, once I reach back, you'll get it. Bye." She replied not only in confidence, but also with full of arrogance creating much more fear in me than what I had before.

It was for the first time I had initiated a talk with a girl hoping it would be a great practice but subsequent to the call, I was completely astonished to hear rather got annoyed and wanted my party men to go ahead without her photograph. But then, I stopped thinking about her tone, her curt behaviour, after all, I knew my seniors won't allow me.

I had to wait not for few minutes but for more than four hours.

After four and half hours, I again called though I was warned but I did, "Hello madam! You want us to wait for two more hours, we can!"

"Oh shit! I forgot, give me five minutes," she replied.

(I am sorry I am not being sexist but what do we say?)

After waiting for so long, we received a photograph in a "floral dress" for the posters meant for elections.

I wondered, "How can I let this photograph to be put in a party's poster, but then she looked smokin hot!" (Not to forget, in the photograph.)

I imagined and thought she would be tall, sexy, and beautiful.

The posters became impertinent, who the hell was thinking about the posters! All I wanted at that time was to know who she is and how she looks.

It was for the first time I clicked with a girl in such a manner, I experienced something different, not usual, unfamiliar, but yet so beautiful. Unfortunately, fortunately, the feeling was never of love, but was surely too special.

In a week's time, there was a special meeting of the party that was to be held in the Physics department.

The day of the meeting arrived.

A girl entered, accompanied by one of the well-known members of the party. I had no idea who was our Vice-President, until I met her. Someone among the members introduced her to me.

"She is the Vice-President."

She smiled; I smiled.

"Who says that first impression is the last impression; today I believed that the first impression is always an illusion rather on the contrary impression is an illusion."

How could an impression's effect last and remain the same?

How could the first impression be the last and the last impression be the first?

Illusion is what I call an impression both unrealistic by definition.

Illusion is what we live in and thereafter, we believe in. So, impression is nothing but an illusion.

Thus, for a start, I was completely disappointed as it was completely opposite of what I had thought. She neither was tall nor sexy, but indeed was beautiful. She was short, super cute, amazingly untied hair, watch on her wrist. Man! She was the supreme form of cuteness but again in a 'floral dress'. I believe she's so fond of flowers that she wants them on her body too.

God! It wasn't easy; trust me, to resist watching her.

Unfortunately, fortunately, she was sitting beside me. We were discussing the events we had executed and the ones we were to execute.

I asked, "Any suggestions."

She replied, "I don't know much about politics. I am there whenever you guys need me."

A shock again, the same girl again!

With elections nearby, such kind of statement definitely posed a dilemma.

I said to myself, "Is she the right choice for the Vice-President?"

Nonetheless, nothing was in my mandate, after few days there was protest that was to be held by us.

(The day of the protest)

I reached.

What I saw was the only girl among so many guys. It was her. She was in a white salwar kameez and black coat, adding more grace to the legal attire. A cute law student, she seemed to be an absolute choice for protest to drive everyone's attention.

I realized she was right in saying that I will be there wherever you guys need me.

But she wasn't required.

Who the hell called her? (Idiot!)

As I was astonished, I went to her and said, "Hi, cuto! We aren't playing *Kho-Kho* here. It might turn violent."

"You save me, in case it gets...," she said smiling.

I am not a Superman, I thought.

But it had engendered in me a feeling of 'superrrman' and I thought, "Are you alright, boy? Stay on the ground...yes, right there, right there! Nothing is happening; it is just a chit chat."

Everything started to turn upside down for me during these meetings and the press conferences that were held in the University Café House.

I think these were meetings that bonded us well.

Again, after few days, a meeting was held and again unfortunately, fortunately she was sitting next to me.

Amidst meeting, she messaged, my phone vibrated at the loudest (*grrrrrrrr…..*) and everybody started looking at me. We were supposed to switch off our phones. And I hadn't. Everyone looked with suspicion as if a crime had been committed; their eyes implied "What do you think of yourself Mr. President?"

I ignored.

"From the day she indirectly directly entered my life she had taught me the art to ignore."

Though, 'ignoring' in politics is like murdering your aspirations of becoming a good politician. In the dictionary of politics, there is no room for the word 'ignore', but still I learnt, as I was not all sceptic that someday and somewhere it will help my cause.

She got up, asked, "When will the meeting finish? We aren't discussing anything worthy."

I replied, "It is important and it might take time."

She said, "I have work. May I leave?"

I said, "Sure, your work is done."

She stood, and said, "I am leaving guys; I have some work, take care."

Also, what she did was, she dropped a message on my phone which read, "See me downstairs, I am completely bored. I am waiting for you downstairs, please come quickly."

I replied, "You lied, and you haven't left. Anyways, I will have to be here until everybody leaves."

She said, "I am downstairs."

Somehow, I didn't want to miss this chance and so I managed to leave the meeting, making some excuses to the other members.

(Mission downstairs…She is waiting! She is waiting!)

The moment I reached, the first thing she said, "I am hungry."

(It was for the first time we were meeting like this. So I ensured I shouldn't forget etiquette, which I had learnt for this very day)

I, less like a gentleman and more like a waiter, "What do you want to have, madam? I will get it for you."

She said, "Not here."

I asked, "How have you come?"

She replied, "I did come with my younger brother. He called me just a minute back. I have told him that I will come home by myself. So, you will have to drop me."

(She was too confident that I didn't know what to say.)

I simply said, "Oh yes! Sure."

We left the university and reached a café.

While we were talking, something vibrated.

Her phone on the table. Message.

We read, "Where are you? Sonam is here. Let's go out somewhere together."

She texted, "I'm in a meeting."

"What meeting? I was also there, with who are you?" Received another message.

She replied, "We are discussing some election strategies. With Shaurya."

He texted, "Text me the place, we are coming."

I wondered what was happening, but then the last message revealed the entire story. It was her brother.

Though, honestly I didn't want them to come as I was happy about something I didn't know what the reason was, but had no authority to stop them.

After five minutes, her brother entered.

Cold looks, manifested me a big question

"WTF are you doing with my little sister that too not in university but in a café?"

I never even thought my newly learnt art i.e. to 'ignore' will help me in such a way and that without more ado helped me and so 'I ignored' and kept on brewing in the brews. The situation was unpleasant and uncomfortable, but then a glimpse of table, a snooker table. It was the only one thing that made me comfortable in the whole ambience, but before I could be more uncomfortable, her brother challenged me for a game of chess.

"Nobody can beat me," said her brother.

Now a matter of self-respect.

I said, "Game on!"

Indeed, he was a very good player, but before, I could say checkmate, and win, he said, "I am getting a call. I am in a hurry. I need to rush."

I thought, but couldn't say, "What a looser, can't even digest his defeat."

But the motive achieved.

This win helped me to drive a beautiful sweet smile on my girl's face, which had captivated my heart, body, mind, and soul.

(Mission accomplished; focus back on the girl.)

I asked her if she would like to have anything.

She said, "I can't. I am not supposed to have outside food."

After listening, I lacked courage to ask her when she didn't want to eat, then why she had accompanied me here.

While me myself wanted to be with her.

No complain, with all gain! It goes without saying that I too wanted to spend maximum time with this beautiful, tiny little, super cute doll.

Chapter 2

Love is in the air

The busy nature of the elections and the schedule proved me that nothing was going as per the plan. This realization well ensured that the feelings should disappear before they appear in concrete form.

The campaigning was in full swing and the complete focus was back on the elections and to win them. And hence, the feelings seemed to disappear, 'but', the moment same girl calls you by your name, with a smile on her face, you seem to fall in love all over again.

I was in one of the department all in readiness, with my speech prepared in my pockets and was just about to move. Voice came, "Shaurya, wait, they are sending me to some other department, I don't know why. I don't know anyone there. Take me along. I'll be bored all alone."

Her idea of getting bored was rather becoming a cause of my digression.

"How do you face these major impediments in life?" I asked myself.

Pat came the reply, "She can't be an impediment."

(New session: Admission time...)

There were teams to be divided again. One of our senior leaders was present there for allocating teams. I wished, I even prayed, "God do not put her in my team." I repeated this verse for hundreds and thousands of times. And, I somehow had a belief God will listen to me.

Unfortunately, fortunately, he didn't. She was again *(smiling)* in my team.

I looked into sky and was wondering, "God! What do you want from me? You really think I can contest in this way for my election or you want me to be drooling around just like a modern Ranjha!"

The whole idea of her being in my team was not at all in sync with my objectives.

It was a one-hour vigorous campaigning. I was firm and had made up my mind, come what may, I will not lose focus, and will continue to campaign, at least until five in the evening, but how dare I forget that I wasn't the only one in my team. At 12 noon, she came very close making me nervous when she whispered in my ears, "Hungry Kya?"

I thought, "Bloody hell! I am really tensed and doing some serious work and she's thinking of 'Dominos'."

She said at 12 noon, but I didn't respond till 12:30 and avoided her, as if I didn't hear what she said. At 12:30 there came a voice full of anger, "You can't take me out for food, perfect! What kind of a President you are?"

I was annoyed, angry, but seriously not hungry.

I hate when people dictate terms to me. It is I now and forever. I hate when I am told to do anything. I do things with my consent, without compulsion.

But I have failed to understand why I was helpless every time she said anything?

I had to do whatever she says not by compulsion but by choice.

I had no 'courage' to refuse her. There was no denying the fact that she is not only damn cute, but she has been campaigning only along with me.

(So I chose the closest place)

Thereafter, we went out for lunch at Gopals restaurant, as it was the nearest eatery and she even liked the food there.

At once, I had an isolated kind of feeling, as everyone around was under immense stress and burden of elections and we were still finding some stupid reasons just to be together and spend more time.

But it did not have much impact as I had learnt the art to ignore.

Hence, the feelings were ignored.

But, I was angry as it wasn't appropriate for us to roam like that and also disliked the helpless environment, where I was pursuing rules laid by her and so while moving out; I had a way to make sure she didn't wish to go anywhere else with me.

I played a prank, all in zest, so that I could make her feel annoyed.

We moved out of the restaurant and sat in the car. I acted as if something is wrong and the car is not starting.

I said, "I'll push the car, you know how to drive."

She replied on expected lines and a much awaited response came, "I don't even know the ABC of driving."

I said, "Then I guess you need to push and I will try to start."

Enjoying the sight through the rear view, I found she was sweating, huffing-puffing, exasperated, slamming the car, pushing, and kicking out of anger, after five minutes of extreme evident hard work.

I was gratified and fully contented at the outcome of my master plan, but she was too sweet that I couldn't continue such a feast for my eyes.

I came out and said, "There is nothing wrong with the car, it's perfect."

Without saying a single word, emoting well through her anger, just on the verge of tears…I was worried of her crying in front of me because if she would have, I doubted my vulnerability at the sight.

She sat in the car though; she looked exceptionally beautiful, cheeks flushed red, eyes wide open with anger and looking outside the window.

"You might be angry and resentful for my behaviour, but your *'scent'* should captivate and end the resent. But, I'll not forget to mention, anger suits you, makes you prettier than usual," I said stealing glances at her.

She looked at me, smiled and problem solved.

We were back in the university.

Unfortunately, fortunately, our senior leaders were on the round, and we were able to reach the concerned department just a minute before them.

They asked us how the campaigning was going, trying to notify the response.

I am indeed a very honest person and so was about to tell them we weren't here, we were out for lunch, but before I could say she shoots out a response, "It's going pretty good, rather awesome."

I was again stunned, speechless and thought which world I am living in. She is so comfortable with lies, again something that I hate the most.

We are opposites.

But as they say, opposites attract. (Just a mere thought that leaves a smile.)

Then I knew she is there with me until five and after five, I can invest my time in the best possible manner. I was happy about this. I thought that would be the best time to work. I can go to the hostels, canteen, talk with the students personally, but I didn't have any clue that my happiness was short lived, and had no longevity.

My curiosity had no bounds; various questions crossed my mind.

Is she all that free? She doesn't have to prepare for law?

Is she not feeling sleepy?

In less than two hours I received more thirty calls that I choose to ignore. There is certain power of resistance and I was lacking that power. After ignoring her calls for nearly two hours, I finally gave in, picked up, and answered. She talked and talked for nearly two hours as if that was some kind of revenge for not picking up before.

All this distracted me from what I was supposed to do, but I must confess, I loved and was enjoying all of this.

Next day, it was a funny morning, with a funny surprise, with some funny words, spoken by not so funny lady. She said, "I never liked the idea of being into politics or even being linked to politics, even though my family is completely involved in the same. I am politically inclined because of my family, but I have never been passionate about it. With you, it's altogether different, a new experience and I like it. Maybe not the politics, maybe the campaigning part of it."

I was completely flabbergasted, stunned and was thinking, "WTF is she talking?"

It was funny and I had no courage to ask her because she is super cute and all is well with her, but I dared ask myself, "When did I saw her doing the campaigning?"

She lands up right in front of my face, every morning at eight and she says everybody will be busy until ten, so let's sit somewhere and talk. After ten, campaigning for an hour, she is hungry and doesn't want to come back until four in the evening. By four, she says almost seventy percent of the classes are off. Who the hell won't enjoy this kind of campaigning?

(At times, I even thought, I hope it is not an attempt of parties in opposition to divert me from the elections.)

Quite unbelievable, how could she say something like that.

Isn't she aware that she isn't doing anything?

During this talk with myself, I have realized that my party, party men, everyone is heavily relying on me and, somehow, I felt, I was betraying the trust, which they had shown in me as their future President.

I was running away from my responsibilities.

(My mind was resisting, wrestling with thoughts, trying its best to be firm and focused.)

How do I tackle this? What do I do?

Then, I told her to get into the serious mode of campaigning.

And the answer followed, "Oh yes! Why not? That is what we are here for."

I wondered if we were here only for breakfast and lunch, is it some kind of a joke, and is she so innocent?

I murmured, "I hope she is."

She continued, "What are the soft hours of campaigning?"

I seriously wanted to know what she really meant. Then I made my own meaning.

I said, "In the evening and at night, specifically at night, we need to be present but, there is not much of work, we will get free by ten at the max."

(I didn't know by any stretch of imagination, I was giving an invitation to the sleepless nights ahead.)

Then we got busy and today, she didn't even say, 'Hungry Kya.'

I was surprised as I was accustomed to it, but happy. She wasn't working, but neither was she disturbing. It was nine at night.

The phone rang.

A voice followed…

"I told mom, I'll be staying in the hostel with my friend for next few days, until the elections. So, could you pick me up from the hostel, and do it, as soon as possible, we are not allowed after 9:30 p.m. and it's already 9?"

Before, I could say anything...

"I am ready. Bye."

By now, I was thinking more and doing less, I was again in talking mode with my mind, "Why the heck she wants to meet? The entire day we were together. At 9 p.m., boss! I am feeling tried, sleepy. Never mind, I'll meet her for fifteen minutes."

I reached outside her hostel.

She is amazingly cute, sorry super cute and then is so well dressed, beautiful and seemed as if she is ready to go out for a party. I thought and started praying, hope she doesn't have any such plans.

She came, sat in the car, and simply said, "Let's move up the hills."

I looked at her; I looked at myself in the mirror.

I had no answer and nothing to say.

(Helpless)

Unarguably undoubtedly, she looked from super cute to really beautiful! And so, I was ready to move anywhere.

Without keeping the enormity of the situation in mind and keeping aside the factors like longevity, predominantly, we kept on meeting and effectively, stopped using our brains, and started following our hearts, which we accept is emotional, but rarely wrong.

The same process of meeting at night repeated the next day and again followed the next day, and again next day and the day after until that night, when we were about to die while driving from our way back to Chandigarh from Dagshai.

I fell asleep while driving and was about to hit the median, she pulled and shouted, "Hey, watch out!"

An instinctive decision of applying the brakes saved us.

She was angry, furious and she said in the roughest voice, I have ever heard from her, "Haven't you slept?"

I said, "Girl! I have been so busy first, with campaigning, and then with you darling. I somehow didn't manage to take time for sleep."

She ordered, "Stop! Take a nap right here."

(After body and eye relief i.e. a nap, we moved back.)

****

It was the day before the deciding day, which is the Election Day, and today was my fresher's party.

We reached our destination.

I dropped her at her hostel. She said, "It's 7:30 a.m. Will you please start the campaigning along with me? I can get ready in less than half an hour."

(Astounded but today surely was looking at a different side.)

"I'll see you at 9," I replied.

Today was the day when there was a sudden change in behaviour, attitude, and lot of maturity. From, leading the rally to everything she took charge of every possible thing, which noticeably sent omens as if we are together moving forward. The day ended with a huge rally, yet again headed by her.

At around five in the evening, she heard my friends discussing about our fresher's.

(Every time she came close, it was nervy.)

One more time she came very close and said, "I know it is kind of strange, but I thought if I could be…."

I was completely unaware and asked, "Say what?"

She stated, "Could you please take me along with you?"

I said, "Where?"

She stammered, "It's your fresher's, I also wish to come along."

It was beyond my understanding if it was right or wrong for me to take her along, but I felt fragile in a sense, I couldn't say no or rather didn't want to repent later, which I could have and so it was as simple for me to say, "Be ready by 8:30 p.m., I'll pick you from your hostel."

We reached the party. Her palpable presence had an effect; it ignited more fun.

That was, indeed, a great night and a stunning one for me. It seemed as if everything was just tailor made 'faultless' and tomorrow who the hell wants to contest elections, when something so amazingly beautiful, which won't happen every day or even once in lifetime, especially for someone like me was happening.

After the party, no going back home, up the hills again.

I remember I had once, when we collectively were leading the rally had mumbled 'what if' I start liking you. She preferred to ignore and didn't respond, but I didn't even had the least idea that I will have to confront the same one day.

It was six in the morning, outside the University Library, back from hunting the demons from the hills. I was sleeping in the car and there was pin drop silence. And suddenly, unexpectedly and hastily she said, "Once you were talking to me and you said 'what if' I start liking you, but never again you said anything. I have been quite patiently waiting, but that is the maximum patience I have. Could you please tell what did you mean by that? Just forget it. Could you please tell me what do you think of me? I have been lying to everyone only to be with you. In view of the fact that I have never believed in love and to a certain extent I even hate this 'word', as no one is selfless and so, love is in danger of extinction, but, trust me, I have for the first time have had this special, wonderful feeling of completeness."

(Unsettled, anxious.)

I said to myself, "Is she proposing? Asking? Telling? Or is it some kind of a lecture? Man! I am frightened; she is definitely making me nervous."

It was a girl who had initiated and when girls do or initiate something they know what they are doing. Even in that case, I wanted to be sure of all the thoughts and dreams that were being kindled.

I with complete stillness said, "My age now doesn't allow me to flirt anymore, flirting won't suit me. I surely would love a relationship, but not for the sake of a relationship. We are no more kids."

She acknowledged, but irked, "What are you talking? Obviously, I have taken time, I understand you, I want you now and forever, and you better understand that."

Though, I was completely unsettled by this girl and the way she spoke. But I couldn't hold myself as that was all I wanted to hear.

I went close; this time she was nervous

I smiled and said, "I have nothing to say but to say. I LOVE YOU Tamanna."

She smiled. She hugged. She repeated, "I too have nothing to say but to say. I LOVE YOU."

Chapter-3
Love continues…

Elated and edgy…blithe and bleak…Yes, it was different altogether, but had the same degree of the respective effects. I was happy as the love of my life has entered and joined me in the journey of my life but today was also the deciding day i.e. the Election Day; I was hell scared.

I dropped her at her hostel and hurried back to my place. We had to be back to the University by 8 a.m. We were allotted duties at different voting centres.

I took minimum time to get ready and rushed back to the University.

(Panic-stricken)

I called her, "Where are you?"

She responded, "Calm down. Take a few deep breaths take it easy. Relax. I'll cope with the duties."

It was nine on dot, voting started, and the clock ticked ten. The fate was about to unveil its cards. The game was on-an

Ace or a Joker. Who knows? Though, I did not expect it to be a runaway as we were fighting alone with no allies but was certainly high up in the challenge.

At 3 p.m., the results were declared. It was a moment of truth. The final verdict. I was crushed to defeat; I couldn't even manage good numbers. Whitewashed by a mammoth margin. It was a shame, unthinkable shame. I was completely horrified.

I wanted to hide myself from all, one way or another, I tried to hide, hide myself from everyone, including her. But in the process of hiding myself, I was unsuccessful as one of my friends saw me. She could sense what I was going through, but she had no words. She was able to see the tears almost ready to pour out of my eyes and she hugged, trying to cheer up. However, she wasn't successful.

It was something I experienced, which I had never anticipated and was completely in contrast to my imagination.

My phone rang and it kept ringing for hours; my best buddy to my love, the party members to everyone, all were calling.

'I lost it' the only expression that settled for me.

But Tamanna, my Tamanna did manage to find me. She spotted me in one of my much-loved park, sitting and talking to the bamboo plants.

Bamboo plant, member of the grass family, hollow from inside hard on outside with stalked blades and flowering only after years of growth, very much like me, weak from inside who portrays strength from outside, very blunt, very shrewd just like the stalked blades so that no one can come close and exploit the emotions within and then I allow myself to function. It is this member of the grass family, which instead is better than a mirror that permits me to see myself in it. So whenever I want to soliloquize, it surely never fails. Rather, it always helps.

She didn't even say a word, hugged me (today I needed this from her more than ever) and accompanied me in the tears.

Silence followed.

We had nothing to say; all I wanted her to do was to hug me, which she did and stay that way for a while.

One heck of a day; one heck of a night.

(Reached home.)

My parents hugged me. They understood the pain and agony within me. My sudden aghast essence was their subtle acceptance. No wonder they know about their seeds. Anyone can or not. But certainly they can to their seeds.

Delight the dejected, and forlorn to fondness.

"When you lose some, then only you learn how to win some," said my father.

When our existence did not even prevail, they embarked the ideas, which were embedded with love, which was for our existence. They produce a seed and sow it deep in the soil for better, deeper, and stronger roots, water them and nourish them as a plant. Plant which blossoms to spread positivity. In this process, they perish but ensure the pillars of values and optimism and the roof of intelligence and collectivity to ensure the seeds must live their life with utmost dignity, even after they perish.

They feed their seeds so that they never turn out to be weeds.

Some things are beyond imagination and undoubtedly cannot be befitted in words. With an open mind, I have no words to explain what and how I feel about them.

I Love you, Mom and Dad.

****

The next day…

It didn't take much time as the moment of truth turned into the moment of shame when the list was out. My own people i.e. the people who wanted me to contest, the party members played politics; they, their friends didn't vote for me I was so told by my sources over the phone, whereas the department like Law, which never in the history had voted for our party, but this time did vote for us. It wasn't a matter of shame because she was able to draw more votes and I wasn't but rather a mere thought that she worked more smartly than me.

I was out of my place for University but couldn't go; I was lacking guts to face many. She joined me outside the University. One might call it an exercise of hypocrisy, but for me going out and being among the same University people wasn't easy.

Her belief and effort reinstated my belief in me which kick started my love from this very minute when she ensured I not only enter the University gates, but I should also go into every class of every department. Subsequently, I was swollen with pride, for her being a part of my life and for efforts put by her, which weren't more than an exercise to face people and accept the situation in any form.

It wasn't now an affair of days but hours and I sustained the way I was, unfazed, furthermore digested defeat I had.

Time is never constant. Gradually, time as we know changes, and at present it started favouring me, it started embedding some beautiful moments into my way of life and things changed.

Until 1p.m., it used to be her lecture time and 1:07 p.m. onwards; she used to be outside my department. It was 'our' time. Which increasingly changed as morning eight became 'our' time, and the essential lecture time, hence went missing.

Day and night, we were constantly together. It was an emergence of a new world and it was 'our' world.

Now, what I love, I started hating, and what I hate, I started loving. Likewise, wandering, dancing, and running around in the pluvial waters, which I hated, I started loving. It was indeed beautiful. Roaming and then riding on bike in the pluvial waters was absolute fun. Muddling and then cuddling. No care the world is watching us. But this fun was no more a fun, as when the world was watching us from some corner her father, mother and her brothers were also watching us.

From then on, they did know about us, our relationship. Problems started. Her coming out of place became hard.

She was taken back to her hometown for two reasons: one is quite understandably me and, the second is the elections in her hometown, which her father was to contest.

(Elections yet again. Victory or defeat. *Who cares?* I wasn't in the scene, anyhow!)

It was in the month of November; she called and was crying it was very evident, it was election month, and her father had lost it this time.

While weeping she said, "Shaurya, please don't ever leave me. I hope you'll not leave me because we have lost."

I was freaked out. I had no idea where this came from, what was this about. I could only say, though I got mad, infuriated with these kinds of words.

I said, "Hey cuto! My doll! I never even had a slightest of idea who you were and forthrightly, even today I am least bothered by the fact what your family is. It was you, it is you who was always important and will always be. I believe you have certainly not known that over a period who I am, what I am, and what I think. I can't leave and will not leave you. I am completely disappointed today with what you said." Comprehend

(These moments were very intense and left me for introspection. She comprehended that she might be having a different opinion about me.)

In sooth, it seems I am a farceur.

It was in the early December. I received a message from her on Facebook.

Tamanna: Please call me. I am out of balance. I only have a message pack. They have taken away my phone. Somehow, I have arranged a phone and I have no balance.

Tamanna: Please call… even my brother has changed his phone passwords, so can't even use his phone.

Tamanna: You don't give the impression that of a dumb person. Call me. I don't have balance, I am waiting...

I was asleep. I woke up at around two in the morning. My phone was blinking.

Three messages.

I called her without further ado.

She said, "Gosh! You're receiving those messages now? I have been awake all night and I am going to kill you when I will come. I so need to talk to you. Everybody is after my life. Why the heck they can't understand you are not an object? People and relations are not things, which can be left for some other things. Things do have substitutes but people don't and relationships surely don't."

I said, "What happened? What is it?"

She replied, "No worries. I'll take care. Anyhow, what are you doing?"

I said, "What do you expect me to do at two in the morning? I was sleeping, love."

We continued to talk and fell asleep while talking.

****

Exam time...

She was back in the city beautiful.

It was she who decided not to talk and concentrate on the studies.

But I doubted for how long this decision would last. And, I was right. It didn't last for even a day.

It was on 7th December, my exams were to start. On 5th December unfortunately, fortunately, her parents went back to their hometown and her brothers back to their college and University for their classes. She was alone.

She called, "Mum and Dad have gone back. I have been badly missing the days when we used to spent days and nights together, I'll cook something for you."

She added, "You come here. We will stay, study and eat together."

I said, "We assumed that we won't be talking and at this moment you are asking me to come! Are you sure? Is it right? It is exam time. We won't be able to study."

"What right? What is wrong in it?" I am waiting," she replied.

"I am not fond of studies and you won't be able to study," I further added.

She responded, "Be right here maximum by nine. Please don't be late."

5th December turned out to be a special change, the day preferably night we were together. We were so up, close and personal and that joy of being so close was not to only last long, but will prevail forever. As what she thought, we did, we lived, formed moments, which were to be cherished for life. She cooked; I looked. She made; I ate. She did everything; I did nothing. She was also the in-charge, as a result imposed her way on me to sit and study. It was for the first time I prepared for an hour for any exam.

At first what I feared, was now more of fun and I was in love with the series of events. I loved the very idea of staying together as it was this period, which eventually echoed in my mind, body, heart, and soul. She was the one I could live with for lives to come.

It was 15th December, my birthday but ironically there wasn't any celebration at any end, an important exam, important as I scored zero in my internals and I had to clear this paper with no internal marks to my credit. Never mind the exam; it was my birthday.

After exam, my few but my buddies turned up with surprises. Whether or not one is fond of surprises, but they have a tendency to draw a smile. But amidst this I was dejected to see Tamanna's behaviour; she gave a very plain day with a hug and kiss, wishing me luck. I couldn't spot that sparkling smile that I have been always fond of. Thinking there might be some kind of an issue at her place I avoided asking her and kept on smiling against my desire.

After dinner, I hurried back to her place, which now was a habit. I reached her place. I entered.

An amazingly beautiful and cute doll dressed in black outfit. Wow!

She looked hot. Imagine what a sight it was a girl looking beautiful, cute, and hot at the same time with the most beautiful surprise a man could get in his life. When beloved turns the darkness of the room into the brightness with her smile and with few candles, the self decorated room and the Maggie huh... One edible I hate the most, but today was the most delicious food I have ever had, the feeling is amazing. The only thought that happened to come back and forth was; how could someone put such an effort?

I was not only impressed but also flattered.

Kehte hai na, some things money can't buy. *Bas yehi vo pal hai jo* money can never buy!

This was the time when we got extreme and close, indeed very close. Something which started with a kiss, led to another and then to everything. These were the most memorable moments I have had as from head to toe; soul to body everything got connected. State of oneness an absolute euphoria... Sheer love. Absolute completeness. The process of lovemaking had changed me as it was another important or precisely the most significant chapter that was to be taken care with great effect, handled with maturity and the onus was absolutely on me.

It was now her prerogative to do and say anything with deliberate intention or with no intention.

It was today when she recalled the old times, which were full of the most exquisite kind of memories and added beauty to the present.

I cuddled my doll close and then what she did was to hold me tightly as firm as she could with trust and belief in her eyes and said what I by no means had heard before, "It was when you were in blue shirt that I fell head over heels in love with you. That was the first time I saw you and haven't stopped looking since then. I have no reason why I love you. All I know is that I love you. Every time, I see you smiling, the sheer reflection of that smile, which touches your eyes, and every time that happens, my heart skips a beat. Whenever we meet, I trace your face with in my fingers so that when I close my eyes, the very first sight that comes to my mind is you. Every time I remember the day I met you, the feelings are awe…

Some things are not said…just felt. Whenever you are with me, our eyes lock, I can feel love. Even if you don't say anything, your eyes reveal the emotions poured by your heart and communicate in a lot many ways than you can imagine. They say eyes are the windows to your soul…but indeed, there is a passage-heart. One look…and the depth of love not only take me to your heart but also connect me to your soul."

"I am bestowed with joy."

My feet. My eyes. My hands. My body...the moment was frozen and forever and I captured it to last forever.

Now, spending time together, being so close in each other's arms was kind of a ritual. We were now one through mind, body, heart, and soul. Every single minute was now linked. Nevertheless, woe betide, we believed might is right.

On 19th December, her mother had a final said, "Better come back, don't you understand girl. We are not accepting any of your crap."

She went to her hometown on the very same day, as she wanted to be more careful now, and not complicate the matter any further.

The last message I received read, "I have reached home."

We did not talk for two days.

****

After two days on Facebook...

Tamanna: When I reached back home, my parents took away my phone. Anyhow! How are you?

Shaurya: Hmmmmm... Okay!

Tamanna: Tell me what you think of me?

Shaurya: Swear sugar lips! You are everrryyyythingg...

Tamanna: Awwww… So cute! This is what I wanted to hear. I am going off line as they are after my life. They want me to shut down the laptop. I don't have any phone, but I will try and manage one. I'll manage something but please you get it recharged.

Shaurya: How much?

Tamanna: It doesn't matter. Maximum will be the least.

****

At night, again on Facebook…

Tamanna: I am not able to locate my phone, but I have stolen a phone from my mother's almirah. Now the issue is I don't have any SIM.

Shaurya: Awwww… Tell me in case I could be at your help.

Tamanna: Wait! I have got a SIM from my brother's wallet. I'll give you a missed call. Please, you get it recharged.

Shaurya: Hmmmm... I will.

Tamanna: I don't know what is happening. I have tried many times it says 'SIM registration failed'. Why the hell has he kept SIM cards, which don't function? By the way I must tell you everyone papa, ma, even these devils are after my life. This younger lad, damn, was shouting at me and he said, "I can't get involved into politics as there are talks revolving and rotating about us".

"One can't be logical, calculative. Love is not driven by any logic. It doesn't have any voice. It is subtle and just happens. One cannot dictate the dynamics of love."

Shaurya: What happened? What do you want to say?

Tamanna: I can't even share. You are such a pessimist.

Shaurya: Pessimist! Why? What did I say?

Tamanna: Forget it! Please you stop thinking. My intention here was to share. Now you sleep. Good night... muuuaaahhh...

****

Next morning...

My phone was blinking. A message. Number was very much familiar. It was her mother's number.

The moment I saw the number I only had one notion "There is definitely a scam."

But it was Tamanna's message, "Last night, I had a very serious fight with my parents and I told them I want to go back as early as today. I will come max by tomorrow. Lots of love. Take care. Don't message or call on this number.

****

Next day...

She called me.

She said, "Where are you?"

I said, "I am going to the University. You have got your phone?"

She replied, "Yeah, I have got the phone back. I told you I'll be back, so here I am. I am in an auto right now, just five more minutes and I'll be right in front of you."

(Though I was happy, but had some important work.)

I said, "Okay! Now that is great. But you should have told me you are coming. I had to go somewhere for some important work."

She said in anguish, "OK! You have some important work. You go and do your work. It is always like this. I have come fighting all the way from there to here, but you are least bothered. Call me when you are free. I'll wait."

I said in an authoritative tone, "Just wait, give me five minutes, I am coming."

We met. My cuddle bug hugged me and said, "Please always support me the same way you do. This is what makes me believe that I can fight and might is right."

I preferred silence as my heart already replied without words, "Always there."

****

On the same evening, I had to go out to meet few of my old friends. Little did I know that a casual repartee awaited a serious problem for me.

We sat together and started our conversation and as guy talk took its route from anything to everything, there awaited a shock ahead, rather a tremor. One of them started talking about Tamanna and claimed her to be his girlfriend. It was stunning, shocking, kind of a blow on my face. I had no idea how to react. For once, I thought of giving him a punch with my complete force but then abstained. It was an uncomfortable feeling, which was followed less by anger and more with frustration and exasperation.

****

The very minute, my phone rang, Tamanna calling.

It was not one of her best days moreover one of the worse days.

She said, "Hello!"

I didn't hear anything more than that and my verbal abuse followed. I think there was hardly a word, which should not be used that was not used by me. Though, I could easily apprehend that she was in great disbelief and was saddened by my behaviour. She didn't give up and constantly kept on asking, "What is wrong?"

I disconnected.

Message received, "What have I done?"

Message received, "Tell me. These sudden mood swings are not good."

I was shattered and assumed her innocence was nothing more than an illusion. I broke apart and broke down. I wanted to be all alone, but the peace I wanted existed nowhere. Even the bamboo trees failed. Her messages were having low impact, in fact to a certain extent no impact on me.

This night followed with no sleep. I thought of nights when I did not sleep as she was around. Today, I so wanted to sleep, but again I couldn't as she was around (Her thoughts, the guy's claim and many other thoughts that should never prevail.)

****

Next day...

Early morning I was anxious, angry, unsettled so couldn't stick around at one place. I moved out of home at six in the morning. I called her. She wasn't sleeping she picked up with a hope that by now things would be better, but before she could say anything. I said, "I want to see you in half an hour."

She didn't say anything. Disconnected.

Although, I had an understanding it is difficult for her to come, but I wanted to meet her right away this very minute. At 6:35, she called and said I am near University gate. I reached there and all I did was slapped her!

She was perplexed, but didn't miss even a single eye to eye contact. She came close with a long face, and said softly in a low-pitched voice, "What happened?"

My cuddle bug tried pulling me. I pushed her and said, "Cheater! Bloody cheat."

She started crying and was loud enough to draw attention of many, which was again frustrating. I disliked her wailing. I came back to my place.

I had to go back for my classes and so when I reached my department I saw her sitting right there in the same clothes. She was sitting there since then. This very sight made me vulnerable.

I went close and said, "You were cheating on me. You are dating someone else."

She said impatiently, "Swear! I am not having an affair. How can you even say so? I have been seriously in love and that is you."

I was furious and in anger said, "I even know the guy. He is someone who is known to me."

The minute I revealed the name, she was angry and I was scared, "It was when I was in standard 11. It was not an affair, a day's fling and we never met. Did he tell you? I don't like these kinds of exaggerated bastards. The rascal would have to face me very soon."

Her confidence and attitude made me believe her or maybe this was just an apt answer, which I wanted to hear. She said that and I was satisfied and jumping in joy. It meant a lot to me. This made me realize I cannot tolerate any nonsense about her and I was the only me who holds right to say anything to her. We hugged and I apologized.

By the middle of February, we planned for a break to rejuvenate and so thought of visiting Goa. We designed this, as everything was perfect to ensure that little trouble, which came our way, shouldn't affect our relation. It was absolute fun with best solutions bridging every cause to leave no discourse. The existing no-trust deficit was no more even a passing thought.

****

Back in the city...

We had a lot of fun and the focus was now on internship. I joined an organization so as to fulfil the compulsory internship period stated in the academic curriculum. I started my internship and on second day started missing her; it was very unlike University, where I could see her, meet her anytime. I was bounded with time. I could not jump the walls before 6:30 p.m. or 7 p.m. even at times.

It was in the afternoon at around 1:30 p.m. she called me, "Hey, busy working?"

I replied, "What work? There is nothing to do. I am just waiting for everybody to move. I am hungry."

She answered, "Okay! So what will you have?"

I responded. "Anything, I am hungry. I would have loved to eat something cooked by you."

She added, "Really! So do one thing. Get up and come outside. I am waiting. I am missing you."

I rushed outside and saw her standing. It was a pleasant surprise as I was thinking of her.

There was a box in her hand; she had brought food during lunchtime. While having lunch she said something that was very meaningful, habitual and had gone somewhat missing from my life since the last two days. She said, "From the day we are together, having two meals a day together has become a habit so couldn't resist coming."

This continued until the villains i.e. her parents saw her with me. As always what they did – take her along with them to their hometown. By now, I had realized that this is the only resort they have; every time something happens, they take her back.

Her attendance was short and this time I had a serious doubt. I had a nagging feeling she was in trouble and to bring her at ease, I messaged her, "I am right there. Do not worry. Relax and take it easy. It is good to be honest and so whenever I am needed, I am just a call away. Take care of yourself. I Love You.

I did know these are difficult times for her parents, but they were making things difficult for me even.

They always took the phone, that she had, away and there was no way we could communicate.

****

After four days...

Tamanna: Hi! I don't know why these people are behaving like monsters when they are not. They are so loving and caring. They should understand that even I can love someone.

Shaurya: Hi! Hello.

Tamanna: How is internship?

Shaurya: Waiting for it to get over.

Tamanna: Are you working on your dissertation?

Shaurya: Hmmmm… kind of yes.

Tamanna: What is your topic?

Shaurya: Impact of Internet on Youth.

Tamanna: Awe... Should I answer this?

Shaurya: Sweetpea! I request I get really bored with your these kinds of talks.

Tamanna: No you wait; let me describe the impact internet has had in my life.

Tamanna: Could you send me your questionnaire.

Shaurya: Why? What is the need?

Tamanna: Leave it. I want you to understand how majorly it has been a bridge for us.

****

After few minutes…

Tamanna: Here it is!

Internet has been a boon for our relationship because through our difficult phase of our relationship, when there was no way of communicating with each other, it was only due to internet we could talk to each other and it brought a smile to our faces and then everything seemed to be perfect.

Now this was the emotional side, there is another side to it, and we shift our focus towards it. The positive for me and the negative for you i.e. 'third eye.'

Oh, yes! For me it is the third eye over you Mr. Shaurya. I get to know what you are up to. All your chats, kind of talks with special references to your special girls, I know it all. Trust me, you are always caught Red handed… huh… which indeed I really dislike.

But nevertheless, I get to see him, I get to hear him, and for me that is the best. If internet wasn't there, I guess dying was a better option.

So, I love you internet, but the sad story is I only love you when Shaurya isn't around. No fuss about it. I love Shaurya and I need you only when my love is far from me.

Internet all respect…

****

Exam time, a repeated torture…

It was her RTI (Right to Information) paper. Everything was going beautiful and our relationship had indeed grown in depth…but as they say, nothing lasts forever. She went to the department for exam and handed over her phone to me.

Mistake…a big mistake!

(Message received.)

"Hey! What happened? Why aren't you talking? You aren't even replying. I Love you! Lets meet; it's been six years now that I have been in love with you."

Government of India had done a fantastic work. I hadn't even filed any RTI, but still it assisted me in some way.

I had no idea how to react; although it was not something, which was new, and I was dealing with such a situation for the second time. After being with her as long as two years now, spending most of our time together with each other, it was difficult to believe so, but the fact was the message was in her inbox, not mine. This time the shock was of a very high voltage however, I gained strength to talk before acting like a stupid.

I saw her coming out smiling from the examination hall. As restlessness engulfed me completely, I urged her to read the message that she had received. She appeared agitated, fidgety and truly unruly. Her body language said it all. I expected her to justify so that I could seize my emotions.

She said, "I now and even in future never want to talk about any of this. I never wanted anything or anybody to ruin my relation. Yes, this guy was my boyfriend. He has been approaching me from school time. I never wanted anything; no relationship. I haven't felt like this for anybody before. Please trust me. It was, just one common friend…it was the peer pressure… I don't want to blame it on anyone, but trust me nothing happened. Nothing means nothing. We did meet only four times. Please!"

It was a futile attempt, not at all convincing.

I asked, "Did you love him?"

She replied, "No, never."

Today, I was thinking backwards and reminding myself of all the past affairs, which indeed I have always defended. I have been an advocate in the past to defend history for many couples, who ever sought my suggestions, but today in my case, I was not at all convinced. I certainly did not like defending something I never believed in, and felt aggressively bad to whatever until today I did. My behaviour was marked by pretence.

I preferred what suited best, to keep maintain silence and end the journey with each other.

I broke up.

She screamed, she wept, she tried to push, and she tried to hug…All was in vain. She even begged down on her knees. The sight made me psychologically weak and was excruciating. The trust was broken.

By now many thoughts arose, mind took the front and heart was at the back seat. Mind had many queries. It constantly repeated cheating, infidelity. What else?

No man! It's fucked up.

Next day, even after repeatedly being told not to meet me, she came. She instigated me to initiate the conversation. End result – provoked.

I shouted, "You bitch! Whore! Do you not understand? I don't want to see you. Just get lost. I have put everything at stake and for what? This! I never expected you to do something really special, but simply be an honest girl. You failed. I request you; do not provoke me otherwise, I might use such kind of language, you aren't even aware of. I rest by saying this much that it is best for you and me is to separate."

Tamanna went weeping from there. I was still and certainly in disbelief. I didn't even like her going away. I felt she should have stayed and explained, answered my question, may be a lie, but should have convinced me. I couldn't resist and called her, "WTF bitch! How dare you could go from here?" She came and sat in front of me without uttering a single word. The matter didn't resolve.

But this eventually led to regular fights on even petty issues.

Both of us didn't have the courage of breaking up, so we continued in the way it was and believed time would change. I tried to absorb at which I failed miserably and she kept listening to everything she shouldn't have, thinking time will change. We were going through the hard trials of trust…but somehow paradise still existed and the effort continued.

Time has the power to heal everything, provided, a chance is given.

Regardless of everything, two things surely good enough reasons to bring that smile on my face and also a source of key distraction when I was in anger. One was the watch on her wrist; I really loved it and the other was her smile. I was very fond of both and she used them effectively in her favour, especially when at loggerheads.

We were together yet so far…trying to be strong yet so weak… finding a direction yet so lost...Who said love was easy? Our hearts had been the captives of each other and the unsaid 'assumed' separation was gruelling. We decided to give our relationship another chance and spend some time together… The most amazing aspect of life is when 'emotions' are understood without 'expression'…words are 'understood' even before they are 'said'…'fights' are 'forgotten' with the blink of an eye and here we know that there is someone, who is going to make mountains move, just to bring a smile on your face. ☺

Though we knew, it isn't easy to stay out at night as dodging parents was not an easy task.

But we managed. She somehow took permission to go in the hostel for a group study regarding a project.

We booked a hotel room.

It is quite amusing when you spend so much money and then you end up not even talking with each other… That's what happened; the only time we spoke was when we had lunch and dinner. As if that wasn't sufficient; the day proceeded towards the night and so did the silence. At night, a sad incident took place, something that I wanted to avoid. As we were about to sleep, I was sleeping on the right side. She had kept her stuff on my side of the table, but then all of a sudden she lifted her stuff and kept it on her side. I disliked the very act and somehow even complicated the simplest of gesture under the shadow of suspicion. It irritated me and laid the ground for some insignificant arguments that increased with every passing accusation.

Every time, it gave an impression that it was just a small reason that could instigate a heated argument; as if we were not on the lookout for reasons, but the reasons were on the search for us. But by no means anyone could dismiss or even belittle our love for each other.

This was the time that healed all. It made me realize that she was 'the one', with no matter how many flaws; I would live with forever.

But it was happening the other way for her; she was being pessimist and I on the other hand, as always, an optimist. After all these moments, the sad memories started fading and love this time didn't slowly start climbing the ladder, but escalated.

****

Holidays in University, so she had to go to her hometown...

During the month of September, I was busy shopping. It was my sister's marriage ahead in the month of October.

My phone vibrated.

Unknown number.

It was Tamanna's sister's call and she said, "Hi! Shaurya, Tamanna di is in hell of a problem. She is been badly beaten and abused. I thought I must inform you, so I did. Do something if you can, but intelligently. Also, make sure you are not calling on any of her numbers. Please don't drag my name into it. I just wanted to inform."

After listening, I requested if she could make me talk to her once.

She replied, "It is not possible today, I am not there. Tomorrow, I'll be going there, so I'll definitely make you talk to her."

She disconnected leaving me in a bigger emotional predicament.

I was scared, very frightened.

Questions emerged.

How is she?

What is she doing?

Is she scared?

Does she trust me?

I didn't know what to do and how to do? But there was a dire understanding in my mind…my inner voice said, "Go, and see her."

The whole night I was not at all sleepy and was puzzled whether I should wait and should talk first, but then the second thought got, which was much more convincing and poked me to just go there…Go! See her!

It was six in the morning. I hopped on my bike and reached her hometown. By nine, I was there. From the time when reached, I made no effort and patiently waited for her little sister to make us talk.

It was ten, twelve, and now one. My patience was being tested. It is indeed a sight to watch when an impatient man's patience is being tested. I could not stand firm after one.

I called her sister, "Hey, you were supposed to... I was waiting."

She replied, "I am in college. I'll get free by half an hour, so after that I'll go and ask her to talk."

I said, "Fine!"

(God! Have I been that restless always? But thinking that patience is always rewarded I begin my self- assurance exercise; Hey you have waited for fifteen hours, wait for one more hour.)

But then two, 2:30, 3 and no call.

3:30...Enough! I had to call.

Irritated, frustrated, anger had taken its extreme form and could have burst a cloud with its uncontrolled explosion, but I tried keeping my cool and avoided it as much as I could.

"Calm down," is all what I told myself.

Finally, at four, she called.

She said, "Hello."

(I recognized the voice it was she.)

I replied in eagerness, "I am in the temple right next to your place."

She said, "Where are you?"

I questioned, "Who else is with you?"

She answered, "Nobody, mamma, papa, nobody is there. They have gone to Shimla. They left fifteen minutes back."

I said, "Fantastic! Excellent! Where are you?"

She answered, "I am out in the lawn."

I requested her to come to her gate.

I appeared in front of her. The moment she saw me, I can never forget the smile that I saw. It was something, which is visible once in a while, but becomes a moment for lifetime. A genuine, true and hearty smile was nothing, but a true reflection of her feelings. I have always been fond of that same smile. But today it somehow added more value. It was more beautiful than ever.

I was ecstatic with quite satisfaction that these moments embedded for the reason that I had come and instilled that smile on her face, but most importantly it was that purity in her feelings, which were now quite evident and clearly reflected in her eyes.

She said while talking not to look right or left and just move inside. I followed the instruction like an innocent child.

As I entered out of excitement, I realized that I had completely forgotten about my friend whom I had left in the temple.

My friend had always stood with me in all the times , forget talking about need and today when I required his support in this risky expedition of love, his guts conquered all the inhibitions and added on to my strength. I needed him to protect me, in case something unfortunate happens; there was always a risk of being caught by any of her family member and the mere thought was horrifying leave aside the actuality. His presence was a great moral support to me.

But then there was an origin of a new problem inside.

She said, "Today, you won't go."

I said, "What are you talking? I can't be here. It is unsafe and moreover there is a friend waiting outside."

An enraged girl shouted, "I don't know. You are not going anywhere. And it is safe no one will come, and in case someone does, I'll handle that."

(I smiled, giggled at her words and thought 'really'.)

I responded, "Listen, this isn't done, but in case you want me to stay back, then I need to call him inside."

She added firmly, "No, nobody is allowed. You ask him to go back."

I said, "Are you crazy? Are you joking? I can't do that. Bye. I am leaving."

She said, "Dare you go. I will never talk. I want you to stay back. I need you."

"WTF is this?" I said to myself.

It was a hell of a problem because I was here with an intention of making her happy, with a promise that the smile produced will last longer this time, but I wasn't able to do what I intended. But, then I had no choice.

I went to my friend and said, "Let's move."

We went and travelled around 25-30 kms and then thought to halt for a cup of tea.

Whilst having tea, I narrated my story.

Complication; confusion; concern; whatever be the situation, friends are there. Yes, indeed,

"Friends are friends! They understand everything and even things which are unsaid."

He suggested, "I'll take a bus. You go back to her."

I accepted his suggestion without any disagreement, but insisted and requested him to take the bike.

In order to make your love's belief stronger, it seemed as if it is imperative to overlook many and I did the same.

Though I managed to make her happy when I reached, she did also managed to draw a smile on my face by serving *paneer* that 'I love the most', making a long lasting impression in the most beautiful way i.e. singing a song and that followed with some of the unsurpassed up, close and personal moments.

Next morning, we woke up as early as 11 a.m., and that too with the help of the landline ringing (*triiinngg triiinngg...*) which, indeed, only had incoming. Smart Parents, I thought.

But the ringing landline stirred us awake. As a result, we were out of the bed and once the phone was picked, everything was in a hurry.

A voice said, “Get ready, we are reaching. We need to reach Manali. Important work. We will be there in half an hour.”

It was her mother.

Half an hour was all I had to freshen up and rush. I took 15 minutes and was out of her place.

But this last day followed by night, had an immense impact on me. It showed me multiple emotions in one night.

****

After a couple of days, I had the hearing of my case in the court. It was an important day and I was hoping to get rid of it, clean though, I wasn’t really worried, as it was a defacement case, one that was levelled against me during election time. I was about to enter the courtroom. My phone vibrated, knowing the fact I might be busy in courtroom, she called. She said, “I am breaking up. I don’t want to see your face. You are a cheater; you have used me. I don’t want to talk to you.”

I was very perturbed with her words. I didn’t know what I had done. I had to take exemption from the hearing, as I was not in the frame of mind to talk and thus, was paying the price for her erratic behaviour. And not to forget her words – it was a break up.

I kept on calling for five and half days. Her phone was switched off. I tried to reach her through the internet, but every effort proved to be futile. She had blocked me from her life in every possible way. I had no other way.

After a week's time, I had received a mail with an attachment, subject was neither love can die nor it can be killed from her email id. I opened the attachment; it was an amazing video clip of 6:45 minutes. An apt song that made the video more prominent rather 'awesome' is the one word that came out. A song "*Main pyaar to vadh tainu pyaar karaan*" which was followed by many photographs from the day we met until today with a personalized video of the moments that we had spent together. It was beautifully done, bringing all the emotions to act together, brought tears in my eyes and only, the three special words - 'I Love you'.

But, still, her mood swings were the biggest pain I had.

It is absolute foolishness to say 'nothing is impossible'. It is definitely impossible to understand a woman. To begin with, she can do anything and everything, and mind it even if she is wrong, she is just innocent, tender and not to forget 'absolutely right'.

My relationship was more or less with surprises and shocks then what I thought it would be like.

Today was again a day that started with surprise and ended with a shock.

It was 10 a.m. and I was leaving to meet an old buddy of mine, and what I saw was a familiar face at the roundabout nearby my place. She was at a distance, so I focused, it was her.

I went close and said, "Hey! What a surprise. Muuuaaahh. What are you doing here? When did you come? Anyhow, that doesn't matter. I was missing you badly though you are always there, but something was missing. It feels great now that you are physically present."

She smiled and said nothing.

I somewhat had an idea, all thanks to my sixth sense, that something enormous was coming my way with no omens.

Her smile was different today.

We moved.

She said suddenly, "I have missed my periods, they were due. They haven't occurred."

I instantly replied, "Wait for few more days; it might be because of hormonal changes."

Frankly, I was frightened.

It was worst when she told, "I have already waited for fifteen days."

"Oh fuck," were the first words said by me after this.

The process of making love was never been preplanned, so indeed, we need to be ready with the repercussions.

She was confused and nervy.

She said, "Get me the pregnancy kit. I just want to be safe and aware."

I was reluctant and shy to ask for such stuff, but again today, I had no choice. It seems from the day I have been committed; I am short on choices.

I went, somehow bought the kit and even read the instructions carefully.

Instructions: one line - negative that means nothing; two lines - positive that means something.

I gave to her and also read the instructions for her.

Next day, she brought it and in anger propelled it on my hand.

I saw and uttered in disbelief, "Oh fish! Two lines, that means something."

I asked her, "What to do?"

She said, "You have already done."

I said, "Shut up! I am serious."

She replied, "Oh really, thank you God."

Although it shouldn't be, but it did draw a smile, as I thought that thankfully I wasn't an acarpous man. I can become a father and in fact, I had become a father. However, I ensured I wasn't expressing any of those feelings.

She said, "Do something."

I said, "Please, suggest me something. Oh, yes! I have an idea those contraceptive pills will work."

She said, "No, they won't. It's been more than a month."

We were under enormous pressure that no one could imagine. One question, what to do? How to avoid it?

Frankly speaking, on hindsight for me, it was a subject of speculation whether it is a boy or a girl.

I wanted to marry her right away, but was waiting for her to say once. I wouldn't have wasted even a second. There were no second thoughts about marrying her.

However, it appeared as if she had different plans.

I requested her to go home, wait and let me find out what best we could do.

I started consulting many doctors, people and my loyal friends. Many suggestions turned up. All too dangerous!

In the meantime, she had to leave for her hometown again. She was here with her father.

Regardless of all this, she had to listen to her father and move back, but this in turn originated many problems.

It is natural for the brain to think in the most negative way when it has no role to play and the same happened here and that too in its superlative form.

Chapter 4

Understanding the Misunderstandings…

Everything started falling out of line, but then it was more or less a deliberate effort to engage in some kind of fights, which may be for a reason of insecurity or may be largely for a reason of insecurity. The hands that were once meant for clasping each other had lost hold ... they were now busy pinpointing the faults and that too on count. Rational… logical…reasonable; we had betrayed these words long before; our actions had never followed any sense and sensibilities. Not much thought was put in. No, Never.

Love had happened. We had complied. And I did not have the slightest idea, even in my dreams that one day it will be all denied…She behaved differently, acted differently, and responded differently…maybe it was about motherhood or maybe it was she who had become different. Her approach had changed and been varied.

****

As she was taken back, her phone was also taken away and she was in absolute isolation, which added to her anxiety.

The only way now to communicate was through Facebook.

****

She messaged after a week.

Tamanna: I am an idiot. I always fight for you and you never believe me…Huhh!

Shaurya: What happened?

Tamanna: You know what! Somebody has told my mother that you are having many affairs and are involved in fights. Though, I strongly objected but the question is who said that? I said he was never like that and he is not like that. I said my brothers are also involved in politics and I do not consider it to be a very holy profession. What if tomorrow someone blames them and comes up with some allegation? I told them this is all 'grapevine' though she didn't try and never wanted to understand.

Tamanna: Why aren't you replying? Are you busy with someone?

Shaurya: What reply do you expect, sweetheart?

Tamanna: Oh fishh! You have nothing to say. You were busy and I was discussing my problems. This is what saddens me.

Shaurya: What? You can check my account. I am not busy anywhere. I am talking to you.

Tamanna: You know what? This is what breaks me. Every time! Every time! I am not a fool. You don't feel the same.

Shaurya: I don't feel the same? Are you crazy? What are you saying? You have changed as a person. You have blocked me from everywhere, changed your passwords, have become a very private person. What does all your behaviour and talks advocate?

Listen pie! Let's do one thing, make me meet your mom and dad. What say?

Tamanna: Firstly, I am not a private person. Got it! Secondly, I have these strict instructions not to move out of my place. I don't know how, but I will make it possible.

Shaurya: I think I can give you ten thousand reasons for what I am doing intentionally. So forget it. I am not interested in any of it now. It was just about what you deliberately kept hidden.

Tamanna: You know what? These are the worst feelings. I am fighting for one person in life who doesn't even want to think about me and always thinks that I am lying.

Shaurya: Really! Seriously baby. You don't have the courage to stand upright and upfront for our relationship and then you talk all this crap... At times, I even doubt whether you are even aware of what you are saying. So stop manipulating and stop using your law skills to defend yourself.

Tamanna: Gosh! Could you ever understand me? Could you ever support me? Could you be by my side?

Shaurya: Please! Don't exaggerate.

Tamanna: Till now. I was fighting with everyone, with one thing in mind that I could depend on you. If at all something is difficult to handle, you are there. It is now getting irritating.

Shaurya: Girl, will you please shut up. You know humans must possess some character. Your mother accused me of all sorts of ridiculous things. Do I really look like a punk, must be a joke. She thinks I am Casanova kind. Oh fish! Really. Amazing people, man! What else? Just leave it, better if we not talk these issues...

Tamanna: I am facing a tough time here. I was not worried as I thought we are together.

Shaurya: Oh yes! We need to worry. This is not the way we can be together. Anyhow take care, bye.

Tamanna: Why do you always do this? What do you mean by bye?

Tamanna: Talk to me. I don't know when I will be online next time.

Tamanna: I haven't had anything since last two days. I am having constant fights with mom and dad.

Shaurya: Don't eat for two more days. Has anybody asked whether you had anything or not?

Tamanna: Don't be an irritated soul. Love you! Take care. I can't talk anymore, my brother the 'devil' is right in front if he sees he will take away the laptop even.

****

The same night…

Tamanna: Hi!

Shaurya: Hey, hi! So, tell what are you doing? Online, so late at night, what's the scam girl?

Tamanna: I was hoping and so was waiting for this question. I asked him to download the movie and I knew he is too lazy to do anything and, so he would definitely ask me to do it by myself. So this is the way I got it. And even I need to wake everybody up at 12 and 15 more minutes left for 12.

Shaurya: Oh my God! I didn't know that you are a mind reader. Great girl! I wondered how come you are so well prepared with answer, but today thankfully, I know, how? Anyway, what is at 12?

Tamanna: Yeah! I am a mind reader. It's my younger brother's birthday.

Shaurya: Wish him luck and also lots of love. Bye. Good night.

Tamanna: Okay! Could you just do me a favour? Delete both my brothers from your Facebook account.

Shaurya: Why?

Tamanna: Could you please do it?

Shaurya: I am in love with their sister and however, they haven't deleted me. Then why do you expect me to delete them? I love them. Isn't it nice?

Tamanna: For now, you delete them. We will see. We will add them later.

Shaurya: Instead, if we will add them later then why do we need to delete them now? I won't do it.

Tamanna: My Goodness! My words don't value anything.

Shaurya: Listen, stop it. Open my account and do it.

Tamanna: I will seriously do it.

Shaurya: Yeah! Do it and good night. Love you.

****

Somehow, these were omens, which I failed to notice. The things weren't happening right and I was far from reality. Nevertheless, I couldn't have challenged the course of nature. I believe the wind of time and situation both were against me.

****

Tamanna: I am not able to talk. I am in tremendous pressure and you are busy enjoying. I am expecting. Do you understand that?

Shaurya: What is with you? What are you talking? I am not having any kind of fun. I must tell what the problem has been. You never understand and start with whatever you want to. When you'll come back we will talk. And I am trying let me see what I can do.

Tamanna: I have never denied about my past, but the day I committed I am yours forever. What about you? You do everything in front of me and portray yourself as 'Mr. Innocent'. Today, I am very angry. You better answer all my questions and just don't show any disdainful attitude. Justify leaving me during pregnancy.

Shaurya: Listen who was talking about your past? And moreover, when did I leave you? It is you who always assume. Stop presuming, please. The ways you fight solidify my belief that our love cease to exist and my presence is hurting you.

Tamanna: Your conduct implies now that I am pregnant; I am becoming a hindrance in your way of life. But it is not that way. All I want you to do is concentrate on what you are doing as that I know is more important than me.

Tamanna: Having you in my life always made me strong but now the way you are reacting saddens me.

Shaurya: For having, I am not a pizza. Got it! What saddens you? Now it's been quite some time that you have been saying whatever you want and all I do is just listen.

Tamanna: Shut up! You know what I mean. You are pathetic. Shame on you for the condition you have left me in. You have ruined it all for me. I hate you. And what else should I say about you? You have left me alone to die.

Shaurya: Listen, I don't understand anything. I have done nothing to insult you nor can I do. If you think I have ruined you, left you or even insulted you, all I can do is to condemn everything you say. I thought I will give you whatever you want and I still believe the same. You have called me pathetic many times and now, I accept and so I request not to repeat. It hurts. And yeah! You hate me. I have known that for over a month now.

Tamanna: Oh yes! I understand. You love me, right? I am pregnant and you are not there. Is this love? If this is love, then love shouldn't exist. You are so selfish. Do you even have the slightest idea what you have done to my life?

Shaurya: I didn't leave you. Neither I wanted to nor can I. I am so much in love with you. But the notion I am getting is heartbreaking. Are you regretting being with me?

Tamanna: Today, you seem to be in so much in love with me but then all of a sudden your love disappears and it has substantially disappeared after it was known I am expecting. Oh wow! How concerned. How can I forget a person who betrayed me at the time when I needed him the most? Moreover, he was busy elsewhere.

****

Mere assumptions of my Tamanna about me getting rid of her and the baby were presumed, where the fact was hidden. The fact of her becoming a mother had given me Goosebumps. I was completely overtaken by the joy of becoming a father. I was jumping in air trying to kiss the sky thinking of the emerging world within us. Tamanna presumed they were hindrance in my way of life, whereas I was putting in effort to achieve at least something so, if in case I was to marry her that very minute I can feed them. I wanted her support instead of complains and fights.

I did not like the words and the attitude she possessed and hence forth, I did not even want to prolong this fight, which initiated for no reason and that too when she was not in the right condition. Therefore, I went offline and did not access any of my accounts. As a result, three thousand messages with many harsh ords and distorted facts.

Finally, I opened my account and she was there to greet me.

Tamanna: What do you think of yourself? Why aren't you replying? Aren't you getting my messages? Okay! Listen, this is the only way I can talk. If you won't reply, I will deactivate my account.

Before she could do so, I did it. I changed my password, blocked her as now I didn't like what she was accusing me for and also at the same time didn't want to fight. Meanwhile, I received a mail, which read, "Someone is trying to access your Facebook account". I was sure it was she.

After thirty minutes.

Tamanna: Okay! I was just joking. My FB password is****** and now I have told you mine. Tell me yours.

Tamanna: Until today, you have committed many mistakes. I forgave all, as I love you and continued despite everything. But, today what you have done are heights, and beyond my control to tolerate… how can you be so insensitive? You don't reply and then you claim to love me. Really!

Tamanna: You have advertised me everywhere. This isn't really great. I am not able to do anything, think anything. Mr. It is difficult to move with a punctured heart. Your body fails.

Shaurya: Listen, firstly, you have of late forgotten to say hi, hello, nothing. You do not even greet me properly. Secondly, you hold absolutely no right to abuse love within me. I have advertised you everywhere! What do you mean? Respect the emotions I have. "Sentiments are to be respected and not to be exploited". So, stop exploiting mine.

Tamanna: Your emotions and your love; Bullshit! I know what you are. I have seen it all. So, stop it.

Shaurya: Please, not again. Just tell me what you want and I will do it accordingly. I hope you don't need a break up which you are very fond of.

Tamanna: To hell with break up. I have been used badly, never respected, and huh! Emotions…they have been walked upon. I have lost so many things at the cost of being with you.

Shaurya: Is that some kind of blame on me? And yes, I have no regret that I was able to protect you from bad people. Listen, my beautiful doll, I might appear to be a very strong person. But I fall in the category of being fragile. At first, I made sure I never discuss what I feel for you but then when I did; it was you from where my story started and would end. And yes, I was there in your home town yesterday and I even saw you with your cousin. When all is fine then why do you message stuff that does not exist? I love you and that is surely not a joke and instead of blaming me for things that I never said...You should have rather told me that your feelings have changed and are not same anymore; it would have hurt me for sure, but would have hurt me less than what it is now when I look at your emotionless, insensitive, erratic behaviour. I also require justifications so as why you had accompanied me to Goa and strengthened the bond all over again? Why that video?

Shaurya: Answer me!

Shaurya: I know it might be all irrelevant to you, but answer me.

Tamanna: I Love You! You won't understand and I certainly believe you won't.

Shaurya: What I won't understand?

Tamanna: All these messages that I have received are nothing, but a bag of mixed emotions. There are so many things, which I wanted to hear; today I have, but then there are words, which only give you pain and nothing else.

Tamanna: I still cannot forget you did not come to my department for my last exam. I thought you have gone back, but you were sitting with some girl in a yellow colour t-shirt. Am I right?

Shaurya: So? You could have come. Rather, you should have come. What will I do at five in the evening at University? I was waiting for you. I thought it wouldn't be appropriate for me to come to your department. Your parents might be there.

Tamanna: No, I don't require any explanation. This is just one example there are many more, but you will not understand. I have done and will always love you.

Shaurya: No, you are wrong. I was there for you. Please don't presume.

****

She presumed an image of Casanova; all was in her mind. She was moving forward with the idea of me being a Casanova. Tide of time was knitted against me. I having more female friends than male was today a problem. Everything was affirmed for her when I was caught sitting in a café with a girl. Again, she assumed. She thought of me as a cheater, but the reality was I was planning a beautiful party for her with a friend of mine, which she refused to believe. I miss days when these birds of doubts didn't prevail.

Tamanna: Whenever any girl messages you, ask you, 'Am I looking good'? You don't even waste even a second to reply. What is the need to reply? How does it matter to you? What do you want from them? What do you think that I am a fool or what?

Shaurya: You are blaming unnecessarily. Why all this exaggeration? I don't reply in that sense. I am only concerned about you, my tiny little beautiful doll.

Tamanna: Shut up! How many times have you replied me back? Every time I get ready and wear something different, the first thing I do is to click picture and forward them to you. But, no use, you are least bothered.

Shaurya: You look pretty always. You know that. Please let's just stop it. I can't fight anymore.

Tamanna: I am a very emotional kind of a girl. For me, it is very simple and I do not complicate. I love you, but it is getting more and more difficult to understand things. I cannot ruin your life. We should end.

Shaurya: What are you talking? I am sorry for every time I hurt you. I love you; in fact, I know I have been wrong at many places, but the fact I can't think a single minute without you. Not talking to you is so much now not a part of my life that if I don't talk to you, I feel incomplete. You are the greatest and the best gift I have received and I certainly believe that God will not take away the gift he has given me; I trust him. He has brought us so close and now he cannot separate us.

Tamanna: Feelings of being relieved is just 'awesome', it cannot be substituted. Every time you say I love you, I am relieved. I don't trust my heartbeats… they would stop any day. I don't trust my breath…

...they would leave me any moment...I love you, I trust you. So never betray me.

Shaurya: Baby doll! "Time is boundless, but I want us to be bonded with time." And I trust my heart, as it only beats for you...I love to breathe, as I breathe to live for you. And in case I was to betray, the reason for betrayal has betrayed me. So, now I cannot even think of betraying you. I Love You.

****

It was her sister's marriage, she had neither come online nor did she give me a call. It had been 15 days now. What made me angrier was the fact she didn't even bother informing me about the marriage and I thought she might be in some trouble. I kept calling on her number and repeatedly messaged her everywhere during these 15 days... no replies to my call. She did not revert to my messages even. Frustration had reached its peak.

****

After fifteen days...

Tamanna: Hi! How are you? I am so sorry I couldn't inform you, even I didn't know. We had to leave all of a sudden. I had to go as it was a sisters marriage and then I got busy there so couldn't inform.

Shaurya: You are a sluu.... Just go away. I don't want to talk. Bloody fuck. Fucking is your mission to live beautifully. Just fuck off.

Tamanna: I came back just minutes back and the first thing I did was to get online. How could you say so? I was missing you badly but for this! Please, mind your words, what are you saying? I know you say out of anger, but that's no way. It shouldn't be like that.

Shaurya: I am sorry... but you should have informed me. It's been like fifteen days. Which marriage lasts for fifteen days? You lie and always lie.

Tamanna: I am not lying. Okay! Today, I want to know one thing. What if something happens to me? What will you do?

Shaurya: Let us understand life as an organ system that work together as one unit. If, anyone organ fails we are handicapped. You have friends who support you, give you shoulder to cry and your family allows you to breathe, think, chase, accomplish and be proud of. But when it comes to love, your beloved has to play a significant role of both; be a friend and a family. That is what I see in you and if something happens to you, something will happen to me.

Tamanna: Hmmm... But I believe it has to be worked out together. If so, why do you demoralize me? I have always been as positive as a lighted candle in the dark room. At times, your words give me strength. It is about love and love...

Shaurya: You know what baby, don't mind this, but I am of a very strong opinion, that you belong to category that easily gets manipulated. If someone praises, you start to believe that person is absolutely right. One question repeatedly stresses me is, how I am different for you?

Tamanna: Yes, I won't deny this. I used to be easily influenced but that doesn't mean you weren't different. You were always special. I don't need to justify myself on this. The best thing is to stop thinking. Here I would love to repeat what you believe in, "Thinking is the biggest impediment in the process of thinking."

Shaurya: It doesn't justify.

****

I was extremely annoyed and upset with her behaviour. At this time, my thoughts prevailed took a centre stage. I continuously told me that I was not the only culprit of various problems and tensions in our relationship… I felt as if she was ignoring me nowadays... Her past continuously bothered me, leaving me with many questions in mind and I started asking her things, which I should have never asked. This, instead, never helped my cause.

****

Shaurya: The only reason that I came to your hometown was because I didn't want you to be sad. Knowingly how adverse the situation can be, it was I who stayed back. Do you even realize how difficult it was? It was all done with regard for u. But I believe it wasn't even thought of. The thing that added more to the agony was when I came and accessed your Facebook inbox, a different you was unveiled.

Tamanna: Please, I haven't done anything. Please, don't talk anything. I love you is all what I know.

Shaurya: Okay! Then, just tell me, when was the first time we went to a hotel room?

Tamanna: I am not sure between fourth and fifth September, 2011. Why?

Shaurya: When did our relationship start? And when was the first time I came to your place?

Tamanna: Why are you asking me all this? And you came to my place during exam time.

Shaurya: Oh! Seriously. Okay, tell me about the hotel, tell me in detail.

Tamanna: What is happening? What is wrong? Why are asking me such stupid questions?

Shaurya: Oh yes! This might sound stupid to you, but it makes a lot of sense for me. So, fast give me details.

Tamanna: It is when we went up the hills and the hotel was... the night you weren't well and you wanted to sleep. So, we decided to go there in hotel as we had no other option.

Shaurya: Was that the first time we went to a hotel?

Tamanna: Yes! Why are you asking me all this today?

Shaurya: Okay! When was the first time we had sex?

Tamanna: I do not like all this. I will talk to you when I'll come to Chandigarh. Good night. Take care.

Shaurya: Whatever I am saying might be impertinent for you, but understand girl it holds immense importance in my life. You know, why I asked all this? The day your friend wanted to talk to you about all the rubbish kind of stuff, you were online for the whole day, but when I need to talk, it was totally insignificant and held zilch importance for you.

****

She did not give; the information that was required… this attitude of her annoyed me every time. So, I decided to go offline and deactivate all my accounts. Next morning was welcomed by her innumerable calls… she started calling me. God knows, how she got her phone today. She continued calling and messaging until she fagged out.

****

Finally on the 5th day, she messaged…

Tamanna: I wonder how bad I am or how cheap I am. You aren't talking to me from the past five days. You are not bothered at all. Thank you for this special treatment. My biggest problem, my biggest fear won. I always feared you will not understand and yes, you will never.

Shaurya: Fuck man, what did I not do for this relationship? Fought alone battle, made sure I fight until I succeed, but without you it had no way. You seem completely unfazed and that makes me think that all my efforts were futile. Today, whenever I think about my relationship the expression I hold somewhat resembles the 'look of resignation'

Baby we should understand "love exist till we resist."

Shaurya: तुम्हें चाहा था मैंने दिल-ओ-दिमाग से,
तुम कहती चली गई कोई ज़ोर न दिल पे,
हमें लगा जब ज़ोर न दिल पे,
हो गई है मोहब्बत सब हद तक,
तुम कहते मोहब्बत तो थी सब हद तक,
पर ज़ोर-ए-दिमाग न तब तक

Tamanna: हमें उनसे प्यार है, ये हमारी खता है,
उन्हें अंदाजा भी नहीं वो हमारी जीने की वजह हैं

Things have changed. I have seized my emotions. I don't wish to share anything now… no feelings… no regret… nothing. I love you, but now I am of the belief this is end of the road.

****

From the past few months, it was nothing less than a trauma, nothing was going well. Our relationship had weakened by many unsaid and said misunderstandings. We couldn't resist our daily fights…I kept calling her for many days. I believe she had gained enough strength to avoid me. She barred every possible attempt of mine to reach her. Sanity seemed an unfamiliar state, my mind was always full of questions and unwanted thoughts.

Has she gone away from me? Is it forever?

I received a message; an only message, which I never thought, would break my heart in such a manner.

Tamanna: I have sent you an email. Read each and every line carefully and understand. It is in the best of us and moreover, speaks the thoughts, which are encapsulated in my mind. These words are mere expression of what I am going through. It might amuse you, but now that is all I have…

"Talking can never be a problem but surely a solution. But, here even talking failed."

Chapter 5

To be or not to be...

Inbox (1)

Tamanna: Love, is it?

I feel worse and I want to write and do nothing else. What I am feeling now is nothing, but sickness. A fear of losing you was my biggest insecurity. Even in my imagination, it is hard.

Today, I am not writing essentially to underline whose fault it is. Today, it is only about what is inside me. I have started believing the fact that I don't deserve love… not even one percent… you are a good guy. To be honest, I feel very helpless when we need to decide between the two:

Your family.

Your beloved.

We commit many mistakes in our life and we regret and repent about the same until we die.

Why is it so we don't get what we want?

This is worse. The feeling is sick.

What I want, what my heart says, nobody listens, neither my family nor my beloved.

You have repeatedly said, Tamanna, you are just a kid and you haven't seen anything in life yet, but I believe the opposite.

They hit me; you hit me. They do not understand; you don't try to understand. I have to stay with them as an obligation. My duties as a daughter have overpowered my side as a lover… I miss you badly because I love you.

You wanted an absolute change in me from the way I walk to the way I talk. I did all. I loved you; I love you and will continue to do so, no matter how you treat me and regardless of the fact where you or I am.

You have no idea how it feels after listening to those words you have used; I should have died. I don't deserve to live. If I can't fight for my self-respect what else I can fight for.

You have always thought, believed that I am spineless, I lack guts to fight for you. But, I know I have fought every single minute for you with my parents and with myself.

Today, the situation is such that my brother calls me and weeps. Everyone says why have you changed? Leave the guy. These kinds of things haven't affected me and will not affect me. Indeed, I have counter questioned that; can he forgo love? Leave his girlfriend?

But, still I don't expect you to understand.

I certainly don't know the effect of love, but it drives me crazy. I seriously have no idea, how will I relive?

I have learned to live with you, and if not you than no one.

I know I have wasted your time for long now. I don't want me to be a hindrance in your life anymore. You want space, you want to live life, go ahead. You are fine, happy and too busy in life to remember me. I wish you happiness.

But trust me I have always been and gone against my parents to fight for you as from the day you have entered in my life, my parents seemed to be less important.

You know what? In everybody's life, there comes one person and for that person you tend to leave everything and become barefaced. Sorry, but I think you have still not understood me and have always belittled my feelings.

I love you 'but' cannot define to what extent.

I guess it's been enough I have cried about... how long should I continue to cry for myself and continue to feel helpless.

Today, my father is looking ahead to my marriage. He is willing to say 'yes'. But I don't understand that the guy I see myself with is least bothered. Then what is marriage for? The guy I considered to be my man has made me look helpless.

I believe it is my fault. How can or rather why am I expecting anything from him?

Are words 'I love you' enough? Wow! That is so simple?

You do not hold any authority to make someone crazy by merely using these words.

The man who has always believed that I am wrong, how will he understand the pain I am undergoing and that too because of the reason that is so very right…love…I hold no respect... no value. What little was left was literally 'auctioned' by the man who claimed to have loved me.

I Hate You…

This is all what I feel now and I do not doubt that it will last forever.

I am not the same girl you met. Life has shown me blend of emotions. Now, I have decided to go away from everyone… you, family, and even myself. I want no one. Do not call; do not text me. Let it be my last wish, please. Let me go away. I love you a lot and it's all there in my heart.

All I know is that I want to live alone and I know it is really not easy. But I want to go away.

Of late, I have started hating a lot of stuff. I feel as if I will never to talk to you. I don't want to see you now. Stay away. Let me live.

I just hate you. Just go away. I hate you.

Yes, I can't lie and the reality is I Love you, but change is inevitable…those who are together one day can see separate routes, on the other.

What have I not given to you? Everything in me was meant for you and all the love I have will always be yours but now we cannot be together.

I must tell you, the fault is mine, I am wrong. You continue to live your life the way you are doing, indeed, it must be beautiful. Some things would never change, even if we get married, I doubt whether we could be happy together.

This is all I have. Thank you.

Forever love,
For love,
To love,
From love.

<tamannal@zmail.com> wrote:

Re: Love, yeah it is...

You know what girl! I love you... you have always been in search of the reason why do I love you. So I shall give you a reason, the reason I know.

I love you for a reason, 'I Love You'.

You are inside my head and my heart is made of you.

Please you also understand, I from my parents have also received numerous admonitions, as they are angry and more over worried about my behaviour. In addition, you know the reason; I have been rejecting all the work opportunities coming my way just to be with you and settle everything before I do start any other stuff.

You tell me, what reason should I give them? I don't have any justifications, as the reason is that working and earning good is something I believe in myself. I would eventually do that. I am not that dumb, but before that, I need you as you add meaning to my existence.

It is strange how you can think exactly the opposite of what I think. Trust me, you have always inspired me to work, put effort and further aspired me to attain my dreams…

I have always repeatedly said to stay together and make every possible effort to be together. I have always used the stairs instead of an escalator for this beautiful journey to reach heights with no hurry, regardless of the fact no matter how hard it might turn.

You have ignored me many times but I don't care as I love you and will continue to practice what indeed is beautiful. It is something, which has taught me how beautiful this life can be amidst so much grief and pain when we are in love.

I never understood when people said 'love makes you strong', but certainly realize now how it can make you weak.

Frankly, my feelings were neither ever decreasing nor were fragile. For me, it has never been a matter of being with a 'girl'. It has always been about you, you my love.

Although, there is no denying the very fact that there was a substantive trust deficit after some unwanted incidents. But what shattered me the most was your mail.

No change in attitude.

I wanted you to understand how immense it is. It is not easy to digest such…

Whenever I tried to bridge the gap, things kept on falling apart as you never understood rather never tried to understand my love… or me

You have always propagated that I have been a dishonest person. If you don't trust me, then I have no evidence to produce so as to prove my honesty. The only thing I concealed was my emotions, but you always had ways to know what I am thinking. I have never been more transparent than what I have been with you.

If you still believe me to be a dishonest person I urge you to do one of these two, and either close your eyes, think of me and ask your soul. Have I not been honest? Or it has been beyond honesty. Or just look into my eyes, what do they search for? Indeed, you might get your answer.

I believe I have done everything to keep this relationship going…gave my mind, body, heart and soul into it. For this relationship did all, gave all. From standing outside your house for weeks to bring a smile on your face to coming to your place in Himachal just to see you happy; I have been there, done that.

But you have lied without any reason, lied from going to the hostel to everything. Why so? What would have I said? Would have I stopped you from this? I would have never stopped you from this.

Do you by any means remember amidst talks how many times you have disconnected and then didn't speak for number of days. What was that?

You lied when your phone was with your friend and you said it is with mom. I believed you. It hurts when the story is all different.

I still remember the reason you gave. You said I didn't have the courage of fighting with my friend. One of your friends even said I was in a live-in relationship with someone. Until this time, I don't know who that 'someone' is. But yet again, I failed to understand where the 'stand' was? And then you accuse me for the so called spine.

It is highly insane. It is not at all important how you behave with your beloved in front of him, but what is important is how and what you think about him in his absence.

Today, when you say all that, it hurts. Either this way or that, I am the loser. Nobody can dare say anything to you except me, but in your case except you, everyone has literally fucked me.

There lies the difference.

And then you say I don't want to discuss.

How could you and why should you say so? Don't you think you owe me an explanation, say?

I completely understand that lie is another side of our life and rather an easier way to counter any issue, but then understanding the fact is important that the moment it starts affecting our life, we need to be honest. But you persisted with the same.

Yes of late I have tried to keep myself busy, but not away from anything. I am helpless. What do I do? I have never been scared of (anything) but from the time you have entered my life, I fear losing you.

My fear multiplies even more when you try all sort of nonsense stuff. I only pray that the day will come when you will understand me better.

Sometimes it is hard to 'face' the reality and 'speak' the mind out, so I am using these writings in my defence, and trust me you have forced me to, as I never wanted to put in much thought to these issues and ponder unnecessarily about them. Honestly, I lack the power to confront them. I always want to see you happy and that is exactly not the way it is happening.

Today, I lost again against my mind. Every time I think of you, your position of denial and acceptance has prevailed.

I am in the middle of many questions;

Were all these efforts futile?

Where was love? I hope not only in words.

Mistakes are for once, but what about habit?

Asking you doesn't mean I don't want to be with you. I need you and I only see me with you, but all I needed was you to answer.

I know the pain is mine because after all it is you, who has problems with me. I still foresee my life only with you.

I would lie to you and to myself if I say that I need this break up. I still yearn that until the time I die, the first thing that I want to see with my half opened eyes is your smile.

You have been my inspiration, my interest and someone who inspired me to get the best out of life, but now please don't assassinate them with your harsh words and insensitive behaviour. Your parting ways would mean and do so.

Love, I can't share this with anyone, but only with you. If I can't even tell you, then what are these feelings for?

Please talk to me. Please be with me. Your mail is killing me every second.

Forever love,
For love,
To love,
From love.

<shauryachandel@zmail.com> wrote:

Re: For better or worse

This is the decision I have taken for you and for me. It will be for the betterment of our lives. I can never even think of becoming a hindrance. I would not like you fleeing away from your interest. Don't waste your time for a girl like me. I am going, going away from you and from all. I always wanted to live with you but never like this. I should never be an obligation but the love of your life. This is my last reply. With this, I will always pray for you. Live the best. Live peacefully, no fights and achieve the best in life. Shaurya, you have been and will always be my ***'शौर्य'***

तू ख्वाब देखता जा, वो अरमान बनते जाएँगे

मेरी चाहत में तेरे अरमानो को राह मिलते जाएँगे

This decision to live alone and my love, both are forever.

Forever love,
For love,
To love,
From love.

****

It was nothing but a complete disbelief. By no way I could communicate with her. Whom to talk? Whom to discuss with? Nobody …yes, except the God. God, I believed in, I trusted in. I wanted to complain against God, to God, thinking maybe God will listen.

Dear God,

I don't know whether it has been always unfortunate or fortunate as I have always loved her and how dare I not. How does it feel to be in love with her?

Only I can answer.

But now I cannot write as I do not know what to write. I cannot even talk, as I don't know what to talk. I have always thought 'good, better, best' for us but what does she want?

I simply don't know.

I have been fucked up in every sense. I tried doing all. Is there something left? My persistence of getting married was never rewarded.

Even after my persistence?

Nothing but 'pure pain.'

Today, my love has left me alone to cry alone. I wonder why I am not able to live alone.

'Heartbroken', 'Shattered', or 'Dead' use the word, which suits the best.

Life is fucked up with fucked up innovations. The whole matter was an illusion, which had to come up with the real image then to surpass the virtual one.

The effect of this has been enormous and long, predominantly, effect that was unforeseen by not one, but by both.

What is happening to me should not happen to anyone.

Today, when I rewind, I don't repent but do regret on my actions. My belief has not only been shattered, but distinctively assassinated, as the girl who loved me once today says, I Hate You.

Today, I understood from where hate originates. It originates from love itself.

The confusion of acceptance never prevailed. It is a simple promise, which was bound to happen.

God! Thank you for the wonderful life. It has been wonderful and meaningful. She added meaning with beauty and this chapter would never end so would never fade.

My hope and belief in you is there and with time, its power will increase.

My belief in you is still there, but my belief in me is no longer there.

जो हो गया वो अफ़साना था,

जो होना था,वो ख्वाबों का पैमाना था

Forever love,
For love,
From love,
Listen God.

Chapter 6

Love in Hate...

A feeling of *"I Quit"* overpowered my mind. When I say that, I mean no more justifications would be outlined. My love was pure and will always be. It is she who has to understand now.

The wait was on, waiting for her to respond in any form, just a response. If she wants us to be together, I will fight the world for her. Just any form of reaction and I will be there.

Though, having thought all this, I wasn't able to hold on to my own thoughts. I need her. I Love her. She is not talking. Where is she? I want to see her. I need to see her. I want to kiss her and walk away along with her somewhere in peace.

It made me clear; I was lying to myself when my mind was overpowered with thoughts, which should never prevail, and my heart immediately understood and accepted, "It is wrong". Do what is the best for both of you. You love her; she loves you.

I had realized life without her is meaningless.

I need her, I love her, I need to see her and it has to happen.

But I couldn't locate her anywhere. Where is she?

All my calibrated and deliberate efforts failed. Nothing came to rescue.

****

ज़िंदगी को जीने की चाहत में तुझे खो दिया,

फिर ख्याल आया और चाहत का जगा दीया,

तो तकदीर ने दगा दिया

We had no common friend; her sister was in the U.S, the only person who could have helped.

However, I got a clue for my riddle when I met her younger brother's close buddy. This guy wasn't well known to me, but politics helped me today, we were in same student political organization. It was he who started this talk about her younger brother. I thought maybe this guy could be of some help. I prolonged the discussion and started asking more about her family members and finally, about her, my Tamanna.

He indeed proved to be an angel in disguise. He told me she is not here and she is in Manali in Himachal Pradesh, at her granny's place. She had been there for more than a month now.

I got up and just said, "Thank you! That is enough."

He had no idea what I thanked him for and replied, "What for?"

I said, "Never mind, take care."

I didn't want to waste time; this is all what I wanted to know for long now. I had the address all I needed to do was to rush there.

After six hours, I was there.

I was fearless and with no confusion. I knew why I was there and what I needed to do. I reached outside the house and saw her mother sitting with her.

At once, I felt I should go straight in but then, I waited for the right time.

After an hour, I saw her mother was going out somewhere. I wondered if someone was inside the house other than her. But it wasn't the time to do the permutations and combinations as it won't lead me anywhere and I might end up losing my chance. No, no point in thinking…Just do it! Indeed, my belief altered its stance, "Thinking is the biggest impediment in the process of doing."

So, I thought not to think and just do.

I went to her place, rang the bell.

She opened the gate.

I stood in front of her.

Her first reaction.

She did hold my hands and rushed inside the room.

I wonder what she was feeling.

Was she ecstatic or was she in a shock? I believe I couldn't make out. Whatever it was, but the faith in each other was supreme and evident.

A firm voice full of anger, "What are you doing here?"

I had nothing to say and all I did was rested my forehead on hers.

From there it was just one thing. She hugged; I hugged. She cried; I cried. She kept quiet; I wanted to speak.

And I said, "I wish for the last wish that I could wish for you. Either, I should be with you so that every morning should start beside you or if not this, then I would wish God give her everything that she wishes for."

(Her silence prevailed.)

"All this time when I didn't meet you, I realized this change is not a one day process. I have come here to just read what my heart and mind says that is 'I Love you a lot' and please never doubt my love for you."

Her silence prevailed.

"People say there is always a probability to fall out of love and I have ensured that every time I fall out of love, I fall in love with my love, again, that is you.

Maybe, I don't deserve you but I love you. I never want to live without you and to be away from you at this time is nothing less than a sin. I believe today we need each other more than ever."

Her silence still prevailed.

"I want to see you happy."

Still silence.

I asked her, "What do I make out of this silence?"

Still silent.

I kept on looking ...trying to decipher her reaction...her expression ...her thoughts...hoping to get some but got none.

I hugged her, kissed her belly, and said, "Good bye baby! I might not be here to welcome you tomorrow, so I bow down in obeisance and believe that you will be the respect of my life. I love both of you. If you need me at any moment, I will be there for you. My heart beats only for the reason 'Tamanna', your Tamanna, my Tamanna. Good-bye! But I don't know how to live without 'life'. I Love you."

I kissed her, took a turn, and went without looking back, but praying and thinking I would be called back, but I wasn't. I believe she had made her decision and that had me nowhere in the picture. She had learned to live without me.

ज़िंदगी के पन्नों मे ज़िंदगी आसान लगती है,

पर ज़िंदगी की राहों मे ज़िंदगी बेवफा सी लगती है

****

We decide, we move; we swallow, we move; we think, we move; we disgust, we move; we acknowledge, we move; we recede, we move.

Everything happens; all emotions occur but one thing is constant, that is to move. Life has to move. It indeed has told us to move. By no choice we could stop to move.

Grief, sadness, fear, misery, pain, anguish, agony, nothing, no words and no matter how many will always fail to describe what I was going through.

I desired to move and move with her; she decided to move alone, but she is not alone as the respect of our love is always there.

But how will I move?

If love is eternal and so justifies the emptiness I am through, I will think and will believe that I succeeded and my love is immortal.

Epilogue

(After seven months...)

I might not be a part of their presence but they are very much a part of my life. The mere thought of her expecting was revolving in my head and furthermore added distress, as it would be tragic in case she has aborted… or would it be 'the' moment of life where my baby has entered this world. On hindsight, it is 'too' not less than a tragedy; if my baby has entered in this beautiful world, even then I am not there to cuddle my baby close. I suppose my presence would have added to the essence.

After our split, I did try calling her several times on her mobile but the call was constantly disconnected. I even tried calling from unknown numbers but my 'hi' guaranteed her 'bye'.

I was always curious to know what has happened to my forever Tamanna and what is it? (In case if she is now a mother.)

It's a baby doll or a baby boy. My curiosity had no ground. Knowingly, she is not interested in tête-à-tête. Finally, I had to do something. What next?

I thought calling at her place on her landline is a good idea. I called. The phone rang…

This time I made sure, I don't fall in trap of 'melody of ears' and rather keep mum…

Somebody picked up.

It was her.

I can't forget this voice; it was this voice that has changed me once and for all.

She says, "Hello"

Her voice again, "Hey! Yes who is this?"

I better be quiet...otherwise she will hang up.

She kept on asking, but I maintained silence at my end.

Finally, in anger she said, "Hey! Who is this? Are you deaf or dumb? Either you can't speak or you can't listen. So in either case, stop playing with the phone and don't call again."

Out of the blue, a baby's cry.

A jump in joy.

I speculated it to be my baby. Tears pour out…

I was helpless, but desperate to see my baby. But the speculation continued a baby boy or a baby girl.

Still in a belief that the baby was mine

Today, my baby helped his dad with his cry. A cry that was much superior to thousand smiling, laughing faces I have been a spectator to until today.

She was still on call and she said, "*Ssssshhh…ssshhh*! 'Shaurya' baby don't cry. Mummy is here. Please *chup ho jao beta*."

(Confirmed…)

The minute I heard the name, I was joyously horrified; joy had no limits and horror as the feeling of living without him… It is a boy, baby stud, my hero. His name is Shaurya. He is Shaurya Jr.

Life is special; life giving us an extra minute to breathe is special in itself. But here, life instead is not only giving me many extra minutes to breathe, but, also a meaningful reason to breathe; breathe in a faith that one day time will change. 'Shadow' my shadow the meaning that demands me to live beautifully. It is nothing but the

"Joy of Pain."

Today, I value why we say, love is the mother of all emotions; no matter how much it, "Stir my Heart," but yet, you are "Still my Soul."

यूँ इकरार करके, जो तुमने तकरार किया है,
आज इस बेपरवाह लम्हें से भी हमने प्यार किया है...